SHADOW PUPPET

and other ghost stories

SHADOW PUPPET

and other ghost stories

Jane Clarke

Illustrated by Mark Oldroyd

A & C Black • London

White Wolves Series Consultant: Sue Ellis,
Centre for Literacy in Primary Education

This book can be used in the White Wolves Guided Reading
programme at Year 6 for all levels of reading ability:
'A Special Sort of Cat' will help less confident readers gain more independence
'Seekers' and 'Shadow Puppet' are for independent readers
'Smelling of Roses' is for experienced readers

Reprinted 2011
First published 2008 by
A & C Black, an imprint of
Bloomsbury Publishing Plc
50 Bedford Square, London,WC1B 3DP

www.acblack.com

Text copyright © 2008 Jane Clarke
Illustrations copyright © 2008 Mark Oldroyd

The rights of Jane Clarke and Mark Oldroyd to be
identified as author and illustrator of this work respectively
have been asserted by them in accordance with the
Copyrights, Designs and Patents Act 1988.

ISBN 978-0-7136-8884-9

A CIP catalogue for this book is available from the British Library.

This book is produced using paper that is made from wood
grown in managed, sustainable forests. It is natural, renewable and
recyclable. The logging and manufacturing processes conform
to the environmental regulations of the country of origin.

Printed and bound in Great Britain
by CPI Group (UK) Ltd, Croydon, CR0 4YY

Contents

A Special Sort of Cat

After Dad's funeral, when all the visitors had left, Mum and I discovered my four-year-old brother hiding under the table. I lifted up the tablecloth. There was Jack, nestled in Dad's winter coat, holding something in his arms. All around us, the house was as quiet as the grave. Then Jack piped up.

"I've got a cat," he said. "Daddy likes cats."

"*Liked* cats," I corrected him, and my voice wobbled, even though I didn't want it to. I could smell Dad's aftershave on his coat, and I missed him so much that it hurt.

"Her name's Mina." Jack said, wide-eyed. "She's a special sort of cat. She's going to help us get happy again."

It'll take more than someone else's cat to do that, I thought, glancing at Mum. She must have smelled Dad's aftershave, too. Her face had crumpled again, and big fat teardrops were plopping off the end of her nose.

"Bring Mina out so we can meet her," I told him, in my fake cheerful voice.

"OK!" Jack crawled out with the cat dangling under one arm.

"Mina's a happy cat," he announced. "Not sad, like us."

A dainty little cat padded softly towards Mum, and pushed its face gently against her wet nose.

"She's beautiful!" Mum brushed away her tears and stretched out her hand to pet Mina's shadowy blue-grey fur.

I knelt down beside Mum, and stroked the cat's warm, silky ears.

"How do you know she's called Mina?" I asked Jack. "She's not wearing a collar."

"The nice lady told me," Jack said.

"What nice lady?" I asked, as Mina crept on to Mum's lap.

"Dunno." Jack yawned and snuggled up next to Mum and me.

Mum pulled out Dad's coat and wrapped

it around our shoulders. Mina's purring rumbled round the room and trickled into my aching heart.

We huddled together on the carpet until the light began to fade. Then Jack got to his feet.

"It's time for Mina to go home now," he said matter-of-factly.

Mina jumped off Mum's lap. Slowly and deliberately, she turned and gazed at me. Her emerald eyes sparkled and brightened as if they had filled with some of my tears. Mina headed for the back door. I let her out and watched as the twilight swallowed her up.

"Come back soon," I whispered.

"She will," Jack told us.

Jack was right. Mina visited us every day that long, dark winter.

"Who does Mina belong to?" I asked Mum, as I helped her bag up Dad's clothes for the charity shop. "The nice lady?"

Mina was curled up on Mum and Dad's bed, following us with her piercing, green eyes.

"I've asked around," Mum said, slowly taking Dad's shirts off their hangers, "but no one knows a cat called Mina, or who the nice lady could be."

"Well *someone's* got to be feeding her," I said. "Mina never eats anything here. She must have a home somewhere…"

Mum didn't answer. She was holding up Dad's favourite shirt. We stood there, frozen by sorrow, until Mina gave a tiny meow. Suddenly I knew what to say.

"He's in our hearts," I told Mum, "not in these things."

Mum smiled a watery sort of smile. Then she pressed Dad's shirt to her cheek, and put it in the bag.

I buried my face in Mina's soft fur. Mum sat down on the bed and put her arms around us. The room was full of purr-fect peace.

We didn't move until Jack came in and started jumping up and down on the bed.

In those first weeks, when my friends didn't know what to say about Dad, Mina gave us something else to talk about.

"Come and see her," I told them and, one Saturday afternoon, they all turned up together. But Mina was nowhere to be seen. I took everyone up to my room instead and turned the music up loud to drown out the awkwardness between us. Soon, we were all singing along together like old times. We even let Jack join in with his recorder, until he started using it as a drumstick on people's heads.

It was only after I'd let everyone out of the front door that Mina suddenly appeared, weaving and purring around my legs.

"Where have you been, Mina?" I asked, as I stroked her soft back. "My friends wanted to meet you. I've told them you're a special sort of cat!"

Mina just looked at me with her bright, emerald eyes and purred even louder.

Back in the kitchen, Mum was making a cup of tea.

"What do your friends think of Mina?" I asked her.

"None of my friends have seen her." Mum dunked a teabag in her mug. "She disappears as soon as they arrive."

"She hides from my friend Ben, too," Jack told us.

"I'm not surprised, Ben's a terror!" Mum smiled properly for the first time since Dad died. "You should see what he can do with play dough!"

"Then it's strange that Mina sticks around when Jack's about," I said. "He's a little terror, too, sometimes."

"Am not!" Jack squeaked indignantly. "Mina thinks I'm special, and she thinks you are, too!"

Sure enough, Mina stuck around for Jack and Mum and me as spring turned into summer and summer turned into autumn. Life gradually began to return to a different sort of normal. But Mina never took any food from us, and all anyone else ever saw of her was a shadow from the corner of their eyes.

"Where did you find Mina?" I asked Jack, as I watched her chasing butterflies. It was Dad's birthday. Without him, the weight of the day was crushing, but Mina was flitting through the soft September sunshine as if she was made of light.

Jack looked up from the sandpit. "I didn't find Mina. Mina found me," he said simply, and went back to moving sand from his digger to his dump truck.

That teatime, Mum lit a candle on a cake in memory of Dad. Mina stared into the flame as we sang 'Happy Birthday' to him. We were very proud of ourselves for making it through to the end without crying.

"Blow out the candle, Jack," Mum told him.

But even though Jack huffed and puffed and covered the cake with a thin layer of spit, the candle kept relighting. Mina's emerald eyes reflected the flickering flame.

"I didn't think I'd bought a trick candle..." Mum murmured.

The candle finally went out when Mina let herself out for the night.

"I wonder where she's going," I said, handing a slice of spitty cake to Jack.

"Home," he said, taking a huge bite from the cake.

"Where's that?" asked Mum.

"Dunno," Jack mumbled, with his mouth full of crumbs.

Winter set in, and on the first anniversary of Dad's death, we went to visit his grave. Mina followed us as we walked through town to the churchyard. She sat solemnly next to us as we stood holding hands beside the mound that hadn't yet flattened.

"He's in our hearts, not here," Mum whispered. She was dripping again.

"I know." I looked up at the dark clouds scudding past, and in my heart I told Dad I loved him, and said goodbye.

We stood for a while saying nothing, then Jack let go of our hands and walked up to the headstone.

"Bye, bye, Daddy," Jack kissed the slab matter-of-factly and wandered off. Mina followed him.

"Go after them," Mum told me. "It's time I said goodbye, too."

I caught up with Jack and Mina by an old grave where a very old lady was putting some fresh flowers in a vase.

"Hello, my dearies," she said cheerfully. "Just tidying up Father. It's his anniversary.

You've brought Mina with you, I see."

"You know Mina?" I was amazed that Mina hadn't run off.

"Of course, my dear," the old lady said. "She's my cat."

"Is she?" I glanced at Jack. He didn't look surprised.

He tugged at my sleeve. I bent down.

"It's the nice lady," he whispered loudly in my ear.

The old lady smiled at him. "Mina wandered off with this little chap on Father's anniversary last year," she told me, arranging the bunch of chrysanthemums, "and she's been off somewhere every day ever since. To your house, no doubt."

I nodded.

"She comes home at night," the old lady went on. "She curls up next to me, so I'm never lonely. She's done that every night since Father died. A great comfort, she is. Father always said she was a special sort of cat."

"She *is* a very special sort of cat," I agreed, watching Mina curl up on the grave in a ray of winter sunshine. She began to purr.

"She knows where she's needed." The old lady smiled at us. "Well, I must get going. Life goes on, as they say."

"It does," I said, and I knew it was true.

The old lady wrapped her grey coat around her and gathered up the dead flowers.

"Goodbye, my dearies." She turned to her cat. "I'm expecting you home soon, Mina."

Mina showed no sign of moving as the old lady tottered down the path. Mum was hurrying towards us. She passed the nice old lady without seeming to notice her. She looked as if a great weight had lifted from her mind. Mum grabbed Jack's hand in one hand, and mine in the other.

"Your dad would have wanted us to be happy," she said. "It's time to get on with our lives."

"Can we get a cat of our own?" Jack asked.

"Of course," Mum laughed. "If Mina doesn't mind, that is."

"Mina doesn't belong to us," Jack said seriously. "She has to go now, anyway."

"Does she?" I looked at Mina. The bright, winter sun was shining through her shadowy fur. "She looks ever so comfortable where she is."

"She'll leave when she's ready," Mum said. "Come on. We should be getting home." She began to walk away.

"Bye, bye, Mina," Jack waved.

As I turned to go, I saw Mina's emerald eyes glint in the sunlight. Out of the corner of my eye, I watched her shadow dissolve into a million rays of sunshine that danced over the grave. A warm glow spread through my heart.

Mum looked back. "Where did Mina disappear to?" she asked.

"I... I'm not sure," I said.

"Mina's gone back with the nice lady," Jack announced. He skipped happily down the path with Mum trotting after him.

I stayed behind for a moment, transfixed by the date on the gravestone. The same day and month as Dad's death... but the year... the year was 1900. How could that old lady remember a father who had been dead for more than a century? And how could a cat live that long? I looked closely at the inscription:

In loving memory of George Albert Porter and his devoted daughter, May...

My mind was in a whirl as I hurried to catch up with Jack and Mum.

"You're right," I told Jack as we walked home. "Mina has gone back where she belongs. She was a very special sort of cat."

"Mina *is* a very special sort of cat," Jack corrected me with a cheeky grin.

I wondered how much he knew that I could only guess at.

"I don't know how we'd have got through the last year without Mina," Mum was saying, "but we always knew she was someone else's cat." She smiled at me and Jack. "I'm looking forward to having a cat of our very own, aren't you?"

"You bet," Jack bounced along between us. "I like cats."

I emptied my mind of all the unasked and unanswerable questions.

"Dad would be happy for us, too," I laughed, as Mum and I swung Jack off his feet. "He liked cats."

Seekers

"Benjy!"

Ben caught the football he was kicking and glanced towards the back door of the house. His little sister was standing in the doorway with her three friends. The fake diamonds in their tiaras sparkled in the sunshine.

"Beeeen... jy!" Vicky whined. "Come inside and play hide and seek with us!"

Ben looked at the girls in their long, silvery dresses and shuddered. He was almost twelve years old. Playing hide and seek with four six-year-olds was not his idea of fun, especially when they were all dressed as princess brides.

"Benjy," Vicky stamped her little satin slippers and tossed her braids, making the beads on the ends clatter. "It's my birthday. I want you to play with us."

Mum's head popped up behind the four princesses.

"Go on, Ben, go and join in." She grinned. "A game of hide and seek won't kill you. And if you keep out of the living room,

25

it will give me a chance to set the table for Vicky's birthday tea."

"OK, OK," Ben muttered. The four little girls clapped their hands in glee as he reluctantly put down his football and unlaced his dusty boots.

"It's much too hot and dirty to play in the garden," Vicky said, wrinkling her nose at Ben's grimy football socks, dusty jeans and Reggae Boyz T-shirt. "We'll play in the house. Benjy, you can hide with me." She turned to her friends. "You three are the seekers. Stand here, shut your eyes and count to 100. Then come and find us."

The three little girls obediently put their hands over their eyes and began to count out loud.

"One... two... three..."

"Where do you want to hide?" Ben whispered.

"I know a good place!" Vicky grabbed her brother by the hand and dragged him into the hallway. She pulled open the small wooden

26

door to the cupboard under the stairs. It creaked open. "In here, come on!" Vicky disappeared into the cupboard in a cloud of silver frills.

"I'm coming." Ben squeezed in after Vicky's dress. As he pulled the creaky door closed behind him, the old grandfather clock in the hallway struck four o'clock. Ben smiled to himself. This game of hide and seek wasn't going to last long. Hiding under the stairs was far too easy. Vicky's friends would think of it straightaway and find them in no time at all.

"We'll hide at the back." Vicky whispered, as she bundled her long, frilly petticoats around her legs and pushed past a pile of empty cardboard boxes.

"Here!" She wedged herself into the cramped space at the bottom of the stairs.

Ben brushed away a cobweb and hunched up beside her, holding his knees. His stomach rumbled.

"Be quiet!" Vicky ordered.

"I can't help it, I'm hungry," Ben hissed.

"Go and sit on the other side of the boxes, then," Vicky told him. "They'll find you first. Don't tell them I'm in here as well." She put her head on her knees and closed her eyes.

Ben wriggled round the boxes and sat as still as he could in the cramped space. There was nothing much to do in the gloom. Through the wall, he could hear the old grandfather clock in the hall. He began to count the ticks.

One... two... three...

"Ready or not, here we come!" The girls' faint calls echoed inside the cupboard under the stairs. Vicky's friends were setting out on their search.

20... 21... 22...

They would find him soon.

39... 40... 41...

What was taking them so long?

"Ben..." Vicky's voice was a shaky whisper from behind the boxes. "I don't like it in here. It smells."

Ben stopped counting and sniffed. A musty odour caught in his throat.

"It's an old house," he told Vicky in a whisper. "The cupboard is full of cobwebs. And cold, very cold..." Ben dropped his voice to a scary whisper. "Spoooooky, isn't it?"

Something behind the boxes was making a rustling noise. Vicky must be shivering with fear.

Ben chuckled to himself. "There's probably a ghost in here," he went on. "A ghost of someone who hid in here long ago and was never found. Listen..."

Ben took a deep breath. "Whooo... ooo... ooo..." he hooted spookily. This game of hide and seek was turning out to be a lot more fun than he'd imagined.

"I have to get out of here!" The boxes shifted.

"Aren't you going to wait for your friends to find you?" Ben asked innocently.

"No!" Vicky said. "I'm getting out of here and *I'm* going to find *them*."

Ben felt his sister's dress brush past him as she barged out of the cupboard.

Good, Ben thought, once she had gone. I don't have to play hide and seek now after all.

It was cold out in the hallway. Ben shivered as the grandfather clock struck four o'clock again. Something must have gone wrong with it. Which wasn't surprising really, that clock was as old as the house. At least 200 years old. Ben shivered again. Why were his feet so cold? He was wearing thick football socks. He glanced down. There were cold tiles beneath his feet. Mum must have taken up the carpet to stop party food from getting trodden into it. Strange, he hadn't noticed before.

There was no sign of Vicky or her friends. Ben shrugged. He was starving. With any luck, he could get into the living room and pinch a sandwich or something without Mum noticing. He crept down the hall. The door to the living room was open. Ben peered around it. Someone had drawn the curtains, so the room was cool and gloomy. Yes! Mum had set out Vicky's birthday tea – the table was laden with food. But between him and the table, there were three little girls in long, silver-grey dresses. They had their backs to him and they were quietly counting.

88... 89... 90...

Ben sighed. Vicky and her friends were obviously playing another game. He tiptoed into the room and hid behind the door. When they set off to find Vicky, he would be able to get at the food in peace.

98... 99... 100!

The three girls turned round. Their faces were grey in the gloom. Ben didn't recognise them. Had more guests turned up? These little girls didn't have tiaras, and their dresses seemed greyer and wispier than the ones the first three princesses had been wearing.

The girls opened their eyes. They shone like cat's eyes in the dark.

The hairs on Ben's bare arms stood on end. It's a trick of the light, he told himself.

"Ready or not, here we come, Victoria!" the girls giggled as they skipped out of the room.

Ben frowned. Everyone knew Vicky hated being called by her full name. Whoever these girls were, they weren't his sister's friends. So who had invited them?

He strode across to the table. On top of a lace tablecloth was a huge, wobbly jelly, a roast chicken, slices of some kind of pie and fruit. There was no sign of any sandwiches, pizza or crisps. And where was the tray of coconut drops that Mum always made for family birthdays? Ben sighed. Mum was trying to get them to eat healthily. Still, the pie looked good. Ben grabbed a slice and bit into it.

Yuck! It turned to dust in his mouth. He spat it out in disgust, rubbing his mouth with the back of his hand. The spittle landed on the floor. He'd better clear up the mess before Mum came back. Ben bent down. There was dust all over the floorboards. But they didn't have floorboards in the living room! What had happened to their thick, fitted carpet? And why were the table legs different? Had Mum rearranged the room for Vicky's party?

Ben got slowly to his feet and lifted up the corner of the lace tablecloth. Their lightweight, fold-out table had turned into one made of dark, solid wood. He looked slowly round the room. There were wooden armchairs where the settee had been. The TV had disappeared, and so had the picture of Jamaica that Mum had put up to remind them of their roots. Ben frowned. Everything had changed. But how? And why…? A shiver ran down his spine.

"Mum!" Ben rushed to the kitchen and threw open the door. There was no sign of her. And there was no sign of the kitchen units. They had all gone, too. The old fashioned oven that Mum called the Aga was still there, but it had a battered old copper kettle bubbling away on it. The only things Mum

33

put on the Aga were her shiny new steel pans, and there was no sign of those.

Suddenly, the kitchen door slammed shut. Ben jumped, and a lamp on the wall flickered. It was burning with a soft, yellow flame. Ben could hardly believe his eyes. It was a gas lamp. There were no ceiling lights in the kitchen, no sockets, no electrical equipment of any kind. The house didn't have electricity any more. This was what it must have been like before electricity was invented.

Ben's stomach did a somersault. Somehow, the house had gone back in time. And somehow, he and Vicky had gone back with it. So who were the strange girls playing hide and seek? Ben shuddered. He had to find his little sister and get them back to their own time – to Vicky's birthday party, her friends and Mum.

The door of the kitchen creaked open. Ben froze to the spot as a girl wearing a long, silver-grey dress glided into the room.

"Found you, Vic—" the girl stopped dead.

34

She gazed in horror at Ben's Reggae Boyz T-shirt. The blood drained from Ben's face as he realised that he could see right through her shimmery form. He was looking at a ghost.

"Aaaaargh!" The girl and Ben shrieked at the same time.

"D- don't be scared..." Ben stammered, but it was too late. The girl had disappeared. The kitchen door banged as a draught blew past Ben, into the hallway. The door to the cupboard under the stairs rattled.

The sound of tinkling laughter floated down from the landing. Ben dashed along the hallway and up the stairs. He had seen three ghost girls in the living room – so there must be two more searching for Vicky. She'd be terrified. He had to find her before they did. He burst into the bathroom. The ghost girls whirled around and their mirror eyes widened in horror. They looked as if *they* were the ones who had seen a ghost. A very scary ghost from the future in a Reggae Boyz T-shirt.

"Don't go!" Ben told them... but the ghost

girls dissolved into nothingness. Out of the corner of his eye, Ben thought he saw their shadows slink downstairs. A door clattered. Had they all gone inside the cupboard under the stairs?

"Vicky!" Ben yelled. "Where are you? It's Ben!"

Ben! Ben! Ben!

His name echoed faintly round the house as he searched frantically from room to room. But there was no sign of Vicky, or of any living thing.

Ben stood shivering in the cold, silent hallway. There was only one place left for him to look – the cupboard under the stairs. Surely Vicky hadn't gone in there with the ghosts? The grandfather clock in the hall struck four as Ben opened the door.

Four o'clock again. Were they all lost in time? Ben crawled into the dark cupboard. Yes, he could make out the shape of a little girl, hunched over at the back. A little girl wearing a princess dress that gleamed silvery grey in the gloom. Ben's heart was in his mouth as he crept closer. What if Vicky had become a ghost? Would she dissolve when she saw him? How would he explain that to Mum?

The girl was fast asleep. Or dead, Ben thought, with a sudden shudder. As he edged up beside her, the girl's dress shimmered in the grey light. Was she Vicky or ghostly Victoria? There was only one way to find out.

"Vicky?" he whispered.

The girl lifted her head and opened her eyes. "I told you to stay the other side of the boxes!" she hissed.

Ben never though he'd be so happy to see his little sister. He gave her a big hug.

"Geddoff me!" Vicky yelled in surprise.

"Shhhhhhhh!" Ben told her. "They'll find us!"

It was too late. Outside in the hallway, there was a burst of high-pitched giggling. Ben's stomach did a somersault as the door under the stairs burst open. Three little princesses scrabbled into the cupboard under the stairs. He breathed a sigh of relief. They were Vicky's friends.

"Gotcha, Vicky! Gotcha, Ben!" the first giggled.

"We found you straight away," the second said.

"It was too easy," added the third as they all scrambled out of the cupboard under the stairs. "We found you in less than a minute."

Less than a minute? Ben's feet sank into the warm carpet in the hall. He looked at the time on the grandfather clock.

"It's one minute past four," he muttered in wonderment.

"Didn't you hear the clock strike?" Mum said, as she hurried past with a tray of coconut drops. "You must have been enjoying yourself."

Ben's mouth opened and closed like a goldfish. "That was the most exciting game of hide and seek I've ever played," he said at last.

"It wasn't *that* exciting," Vicky said. "I've got a much better idea for a hiding place. Is there time for another game before my birthday tea?"

"Oh, yes," Mum smiled. "There's plenty of time. Ben, you'd love to play another game of hide and seek with your sister, wouldn't you?"

Shadow Puppet

"Go, Sajil, go!"

Sajil's friends cheered as he raced towards the open goal.

"Aaaawwwwwwwwwwwwwwww!"

They groaned as Sajil's foot missed the ball and it trickled harmlessly across the goal mouth. Sajil looked at his foot in surprise. It didn't usually let him down. He ran towards the ball for a second chance.

"Sa-jil! Sa-jil!" a handful of voices called.

He kicked at the ball and missed again, just as his friend Ryan zoomed up and chipped the ball into the goal.

"Ry-an!" the Milltown Magpies supporters went wild.

Sajil jogged back to his place in the line up. What was wrong with him? He was one of the Milltown Magpies youth team's star players, but it was as if his feet didn't belong to him. He looked round the pitch. In the late-afternoon sunshine, the players' elongated shadows lay silently on the grass as they waited for play to begin. Suddenly, the pitch sprang to life as the shadows darted away. Sajil took off after his spindly shadow. It was weird! Instead of him leading his shadow, his shadow was leading him! And it was useless at football. For the rest of the match, Sajil missed every ball that came his way.

"What's up with you?" Ryan asked, as they walked off the pitch. "I've never seen you play that badly before. We drew against the Hackford Hawks! We should have thrashed them!"

"I couldn't help it," Sajil ran his hands through his short, spiky hair. "It's like my shadow's in control of me, not the other way round!"

"That's the stupidest, lamest excuse I've ever heard!" Ryan's shadow overlapped with Sajil's as he stopped and glared at his friend.

Sajil stood open-mouthed as he watched his shadow push Ryan's shadow away.

"Hey!" Ryan yelled. "Don't push me about!"

"I'm not…!"

Too late, Sajil realised that his hands were on Ryan's shoulders.

"Oof!" Sajil fell heavily, as Ryan shoved him back. "My shadow made me do it!" he explained.

"Yeah, right!" Ryan shrugged as he turned his back on Sajil and walked away.

Sajil got to his feet. Was it his imagination, or did his shadow move first? He kicked first one foot and then the other. It was difficult to tell. He did it again more slowly. Weird. His shadow feet looked like the talons of a bird of prey. It must be the studs in my football boots, Sajil told himself. A trick of the light!

Back home, Sajil's mother was sitting at the kitchen table, drinking a cup of tea and reading a letter. She waved it at Sajil as he came in.

"It's from Indonesia," she told him. "You remember Great Auntie who died last month?"

Sajil nodded. He'd only met his great aunt once, when he was quite small and she was on her one and only trip to England.

"This letter's from her friend," Mum went on. "It says that before she died, Great Auntie arranged for two special puppets to be sent to you. Her friend wants to know if they've arrived yet."

Mum put down her cup of tea. "They haven't, of course. Parcel post takes ages sometimes," she sighed, "but I guess they'll arrive soon. That was kind of Auntie, wasn't it?"

"I suppose so," Sajil mumbled. The only thing he could think about was football. He dumped his smelly kit bag on the floor. "We drew against the Hawks!" he groaned.

"Well, a draw's OK, isn't it?" Mum said brightly. "At least you didn't lose. And there's always next time!"

"We don't play the Hawks again for ages," Sajil groaned. "Next week, we play the Foxley Falcons, and they always win!" He stomped off to his room.

It rained all Saturday evening and all day Sunday, so no shadows were to be seen. By first lesson on Monday morning, it was a math's problem, not a shadow problem, that was on Sajil's mind. He gazed out at the hazy sunshine trying to break through the clouds. He sighed and glanced across at Ryan, who was busily scribbling down figures in his large, bold handwriting. If he narrowed his eyes, he could just about make out what they were.

As Sajil began to copy Ryan's answers, a ray of sunshine shone through the classroom window, projecting the children's shadows on the wall. Sajil looked up and stifled a gasp. His shadow had grown horns! He glanced down at "his" work. What was he doing copying from Ryan? He never copied! His shadow must be making him do it!

Sajil's heart thumped as he glanced round the class. A few of his classmates were gazing at the wall with blank expressions. They clearly couldn't see what he could. Was he going mad? He tore up the paper.

"Sorry, I made a mistake!" he told his teacher.

Sajil made another mistake on the way home with Ryan. He couldn't stop himself. They went into the corner shop because Ryan wanted some bubble gum, and Sajil's fingers somehow found their way around a chocolate bar... and didn't pay for it. Outside in the sunshine, he watched, mesmerised, as the shadow unwrapped it with long, thin, claw-like fingers and stuffed it into his gaping mouth. The chocolate tasted good. But then, suddenly, the sun went behind a cloud and the shadow disappeared. Sajil looked in horror at the empty wrapper in his hands.

"It's taking me over!" he muttered, dashing back into the shop and slamming down a handful of change on the counter.

"What's taking you over?" Ryan blew an enormous sticky bubble.

"My shadow!" Sajil told him as the pink

48

bubble popped all over Ryan's nose. "It's out of control!"

"Don't be crazy!" Ryan peeled bubble gum off his freckly nose. "You control your shadow, not the other way round."

"I'm not so sure." Sajil led the way into his house and up the stairs to his room. "Check this out!" He closed the curtains and switched on his bedside light so that their shadows appeared on the wall. Ryan's shadow looked normal, but Sajil could clearly make out horns and claw like fingers and taloned feet on his.

"See anything strange about my shadow?" he asked Ryan.

"No." Ryan wasn't looking at the shadow, he was examining the gum he had taken out of his mouth. He put it back in the wrapper and stuffed it in his pocket. "What's the problem? It's just an ordinary shadow, and we can make it disappear, just like this!" Ryan snapped off the light.

"Ordinary?" Sajil squeaked. A wave of anger swept through him. He couldn't help himself. His shadowy hands grabbed the old cricket bat he kept in the corner of the room.

"See!" Ryan snapped the light back on.

"Watch out!" Sajil yelled. His long, shadowy arms were swinging the bat menacingly towards Ryan.

Just in time, Ryan jumped out of the way. Sajil dropped the bat and pointed to his shadow with a shaking finger. The shadow pointed back, and opened its mouth in a devilish grin. Its teeth were pointed fangs!

"What on earth is that?" Ryan's mouth had dropped open. He was staring at Sajil's shadow.

Sajil sighed with relief. He wasn't going mad. At last, Ryan had seen it, too.

The front door slammed. Sajil nearly jumped out of his skin. He and Ryan rushed to the top of the stairs.

"It's only Mum!" Sajil breathed a sigh of relief. His mother was at the bottom of the stairs holding two parcels.

"Sajil!" she called up to him. "I've just been down to the post office to fetch these! They're the puppets Great Auntie sent from Indonesia! Come and see! They're addressed to you!"

Sajil grimaced at Ryan. "We'd better go down and see these boring old puppets," he muttered.

"We'll deal with the shadow later," Ryan agreed.

They clattered down the stairs.

Mum put down the parcels on the kitchen table. They were both the size and shape of shoeboxes. A gash was torn out of the side of one of them.

"That one must have been damaged in the post," Mum said, putting on the kettle. "But the other's in one piece!"

"Let's see what's inside!" Sajil took the undamaged box, tore off the brown paper wrapping and he and Ryan peered inside.

"Is it a puppet?" Mum asked.

"It's not like any puppet I've ever seen,"

Ryan commented, as Sajil lifted out a flat figure made of leather. Its long arms swung from its shoulder joints.

"Where are the strings?" he asked.

"There aren't any strings, you use these control rods." Sajil's mum put down her cup of tea and pointed to the rods attached to the hands. Sajil turned the puppet over. The leather was carefully chiselled into the shape of a young man wearing traditional robes. His costume was so delicately cut that the leather looked like lace.

Sajil stared at the puppet. A handsome face gazed serenely back at him.

"How lovely!" Mum smiled. "He's the prince of goodness and light!"

Sajil carefully laid the figure on the table and turned his attention to the damaged parcel.

"It looks as if this one's tried to break out of the box!" Ryan commented, pointing to the back of the puppet's head that was stuck in the gash.

Sajil held up the puppet. The leather it was made of was much thicker than the other. Sajil couldn't make out whether the hunched figure was of a man or a woman.

The figure's bulky clothing hung from it in rags. Claw-like hands and feet dangled evilly. On its bulbous head, two distinct horns poked out of its matted hair. The hairs on the back of Sajil's neck prickled.

"It's just like my shadow!" he gasped. Chills ran down his spine.

"That's right." Mum had misheard. "They're Indonesian shadow puppets." She pointed at the second puppet with an expression of disgust. "This horrible thing with pointy teeth is an ogre. It spreads darkness and wickedness. In shadow puppet plays, it fights with the prince and tries to gobble up all that is good!"

"So who wins?" Ryan asked nervously.

"That depends." Sajil's mother sipped at her tea.

"On what?" Sajil held his breath.

53

"On who's controlling the puppets," Mum said. "Are you going to do a show?"

Ryan and Sajil looked at each other.

"Yes!" they said together.

"Are you sure this is a good idea?" Ryan asked, as they pinned a bed sheet over the doorway. "If your shadow's being taken over by the puppet ogre, doing a shadow puppet show might make it stronger!"

"It's a risk I have to take!" Sajil dragged over the coffee table and set up a lamp on it. "The only way to stop it is to get the good prince puppet to defeat the ogre puppet!"

"But what if the prince doesn't win?"

"That doesn't bear thinking about," Sajil said grimly, turning on the lamp. "Here. You take the prince. I'm stuck with the ogre – for now!" He shuddered as he picked up the hideous leather puppet.

Sajil and Ryan took up their positions behind the sheet. From the other side of the doorway, Mum clapped her hands in delight.

"This is great fun! It reminds me of when I was a little girl in Indonesia!" she giggled.

Sajil grimaced at Ryan. They grabbed the control rods and held up the puppets so that their shadows were projected on to the sheet. Light shone through the fine clothes of the shadow Prince, but the shadow ogre was as hunched and menacing as a watchful vulture.

There was a rushing sound like the flapping of wings. The ogre shadow puppet swooped on the prince. The prince staggered and fell back.

"Careful!" Ryan hissed.

"I can't help it!" Sajil whispered. He took his hands off the control rods. "It's working itself!"

"So is the prince!" Ryan let his hands drop to his sides. The prince struggled to his feet and advanced on the ogre.

The shadow puppets wrestled each other to and fro across the screen. Time and time again, the evil ogre seemed about to engulf the good prince, and time and time again, the good prince sprang back for more. Sajil's heart was in his mouth as he watched the age-old epic battle of good versus evil.

"Kill the ogre!" Sajil urged on the prince. But it was no good, both sides were evenly matched. The puppets' movements were getting slower and slower.

"They've worn themselves out!" Ryan whispered, as the puppets crumpled in a heap on the ground.

On the other side of the sheet screen, Mum clapped her hands.

"Bravo!" she cheered. "A draw! A balance between good and evil! Just like real life!"

"I don't like draws!" Sajil muttered through clenched teeth. He grabbed the leather ogre puppet. It winked at him with one evil eye as he tried to tear off its ghastly head. But it was no good, the leather was too thick!

"Sajil! What do you think you're doing?" Mum said in horror, pushing her way past the sheet. "These puppets are part of your heritage! If that's how you're going to treat them, I shall have to put them away until you're older!"

As Sajil and Ryan watched, she carefully packed the two puppets together in the undamaged shoebox and got out a roll of sticky tape.

"This box is staying on top of my wardrobe and is not to be touched until you're 18!" she ordered, as she taped it up.

"Fine by me!" Sajil muttered. "Put plenty of tape on that box!"

"Go, Sajil, go!"

It was the following Saturday and the Milltown Magpies supporters' calls were ringing in Sajil's ears as he raced across the goal mouth. His boot connected with the ball.

"Goooooooooal!" they cheered.

"Yes!" Sajil punched the air in delight, as the referee blew his whistle for full time. He'd scored the winning goal!

"Nice one!" Ryan said as they walked off

the football pitch together. "We don't usually beat the Falcons!" He grinned at Sajil. "Everything's back to normal, then?"

Sajil glanced back at his shadow. It was following him obediently.

"It seems to be," he shrugged. "But I'll keep checking the lid's firmly on that box!"

"So would I!" agreed Ryan. "But what happens when you're 18 and your mum gives it back to you? Will you take those puppets out?"

"I don't know," said Sajil, thoughtfully, as he unlaced his football boots. "It's a long way off. What would you do if you were me?"

Smelling of Roses

I can smell it as soon as I set foot on the stepping stones. It's just a hint at first. More a sickly sweet taste in the air than a smell. Nothing much. Nothing I can put my finger on, anyway. It's nagging away at me because it's vaguely familiar, like a lost memory. It makes me a bit uneasy, to tell you the truth. But there's no time to think about it now. I'm late for school again, and there's this horrendous hill to climb before I get there.

Step by heavy step, I trudge up the stepping stones. Way back in the past, someone set these stones into the hillside, like steps, each a stride apart. They're all worn down in the middle. The village is at the top of the hill, and in the old days there was a cotton mill down by the river at the bottom. The mill workers who lived in the village must have passed this way every day for years and years. The old mill's been made into flats now – my family lives there, and so does Riya's. Any normal day, I'd be walking to school with Riya and her little sister, but today it's just me. My feet fit perfectly into the hollows made by all the feet that have trekked up and down these stones before.

Oof! This backpack weighs a ton. Mum keeps telling me to leave some books behind, but if you do that, they're always the ones you want, aren't they? No one's looking, so I'm carrying it properly, a strap over each shoulder. 'Course, I wouldn't be seen dead carrying it like that at school. Slung over one shoulder is fine, but two shoulders? C'mon. That's for nerds. Everyone in my class would laugh. Well, Riya would, anyway, and that would be far, far worse.

It's a 'Sound of Music' morning. The sun's shining brightly, the birds are singing, and the grassy slope is sprinkled with wild flowers and alive with busy, buzzy bees. On a day like this, Riya always says, she wouldn't be surprised to see someone dressed as a nun skipping over the top of the hill and bursting into song. Riya might joke about it, but it makes me sick. I mean really sick. I'd swap it all for the city and a bit of pollution. It's the pollen, you see.

My chest. It's being crushed. Wheeze as I breathe in. Squeak as I breathe out. Like a creaky door you can't push open.

I stop and take off my backpack. Get out my asthma inhaler.

Phew...

It works really quickly. I'm breathing a lot easier, when I hear it. Or I *think* I hear it. A low moan. Just one. The skin on the back of my neck prickles. Don't be daft, I tell myself, it's just a gust of wind. As if to prove me right, a chilly breeze ripples across the hillside. It smells musty.

"Atchoo!"

Great. Hay fever as well. I look at my watch. No point in rushing when you have asthma. Just plod on. By the time I get to the top of the hill, I can hear the school bell ringing. I suppose Riya's already got there. I wonder if she's going to talk to me today. Another day at t'mill – as Dad will insist on saying every morning before he gets into his car and drives off along the valley road to his office in town.

Her feet clattered down the stepping stones towards the mill. If she was late, the mill owners would dock her pay. Or worse, much worse, she'd lose her job. Then she'd never be able to feed herself, let alone this baby she carried inside her. As it was, she hadn't eaten properly since Mam had thrown her out. She'd found shelter in the outhouse at the back of the yard, but there was no comfort there. Tears filled her hazel eyes. No one seemed to care if she lived or died. Mam would have nothing to do with her, not now it had begun to show. And when she'd told her best friend what had happened between her and the mill owner's son, her best friend had stopped speaking to her. As for the mill owner's son, it was as if she'd never even existed. The future looked grim. As grim as the smoke that billowed from the mill chimneys and hung over the valley beneath her. Better not to think of it now. She wiped away the tears with her sleeve and sniffed loudly. Her lungs filled with the sweet scent of the wild roses that lined the steep path. She began to cough, and as she gasped and spluttered, a wave of nausea broke over her. She choked it back. Can't be late, can't be late. Her clogs beat out a desperate rhythm as she clattered down the stepping stones.

School's started by the time I get there. Everyone looks up as I open the classroom door.

"It's the hill, miss," I gasp as I slide behind my desk. "I couldn't climb it fast enough because of my asthma!"

Old Ma Harding looks down her nose at me, says she's sorry about the asthma, but she wasn't born yesterday, and that I should try getting up earlier for a change. Then she wrinkles her nose and announces: "There's a strange odour in this classroom!"

She squeezes past my desk, looking at me as if I'm the source of the bad smell, and opens the window next to me.

In wafts that musty scent and makes a bee-line for my nose.

"Atchoo!"

"Bless you!" everyone yells, but not Riya. My ex-best friend still isn't talking to me.

She's really mad because I went to Alex's birthday party on Saturday. Alex invited me, you see – but he didn't invite Riya. According to Riya, I should have gone round to her flat instead, and told Alex to stuff his invitation. She won't speak to me now. Maybe she'll forgive me one day. Or maybe she'll never talk to me again. Either way, I don't think things will ever be the same between us, so it looks as if we both need to find a new best friend. It's not as if the party was much good, either – all we did was sit around watching DVDs while the boys talked football. Boring.

I sigh, and the sigh fills my nose with fusty, musty dust...

"Atchoo!"

"Bless you!" everyone but Riya yells again.

Ma Harding remarks that the fragrance of roses doesn't seem to suit me, which, she says, all things considered, is curious.

Only Riya laughs, but it isn't a very nice laugh.

Roses? It doesn't smell like any roses I've ever come across. Not like Dad's roses –

they're his favourite flower. I should know, he's always telling me. And everyone tells me that Dad's roses smell gorgeous, even though I've never dared bury my nose in them and take a good, deep sniff.

This smell is fusty. If it is roses, then they must have that disgusting rotting disease where the petals turn sludgy and slimy before they dry out. Mildew, Dad calls it. Mildewed roses. Ugh! Whatever it is, it's getting right up my nose. I'm going to sneeze again...

"A... at... choo!"

She couldn't help sneezing, but sneezing didn't clear her nose. It just made her inhale more dust. Fine, powdery, choking dust. Cotton dust. Inside the mill, it was everywhere, blanketing the floor, hanging in the air, clogging up the machinery and the workers' lungs. Not that the mill owners cared about the workers' lungs. Not that there was any medicine that would help the workers if they did. The roar of the huge machines drowned out her sneezes. No one said "bless you", but then again, no one was speaking to her these days. In any case, she didn't think she deserved to be blessed. A sudden racking cough bent her double. She straightened up, thumping her breastbone as she caught her breath. Then she ran her hands through her long, straggly blonde hair, and pushed it away from her face. Even inside the smoky mill, it smelled of roses.

Funny things, smells. When they've been around for a while, you stop noticing them. Well, most smells. Not farts. Some of the boys at Alex's party were boasting they could fart to order and, believe me, you could smell that for ever. But most smells, they're there but not there, if you see what I mean. Like the mildewed roses. They're there, lurking in the background, but I manage to put them out of my mind for the rest of the morning. Ma Harding's talking about the Industrial Revolution, and for once everyone's paying attention because she's telling us what it was like in the old cotton mill.

It was terrible! Kids as young as four years old had to work down there, spinning and weaving, making cloth, for twelve hours every day except Sunday, and they got hardly any money for it. The mill was jam-packed with machines that ran on coal, so the whole valley was filled with filthy smoke, and the work was really dangerous – the workers got caught up in machines, or got chest diseases because their lungs got clogged with dust. And there weren't any medicines, or they couldn't afford what medicines there were, so lots of them died young.

As Ma Harding tells us about it, I'm imagining I'm there. Pictures and feelings flood my mind like someone else's memories.

I'm lost in time, so time passes quickly until the school bell rings and jolts me back to reality. It's lunch. Every Monday, school dinner is pizza or dog-sick-on-a-frisbee, as Riya and I call it. Then we make gagging noises and fall around giggling until the dinner ladies tell us off. The thought makes me smile, then this awful, empty feeling washes over me. I'm not hungry. But the empty feeling doesn't have anything to do with my stomach being empty, it's got everything to do with having lost my best friend.

Riya's over there, sitting at our table as if it's an ordinary Monday, only she's giggling and making gagging noises with someone else, not me. Perhaps I should sit at Alex's table and pretend to laugh and joke with him, but his table's full of boys talking football. They're the same boys who were at his horrible birthday party.

In the end, I decide to go outside to avoid Monday pizza, and all the boys who remind me of Alex's party. Most of all, I go outside to avoid the sight of my ex-best friend Riya making a new best friend. But once I'm outside, there's no avoiding the smell of mildewed roses. The playground reeks of them. I peer through the fence looking for roses, any kind of roses, but there are none to be seen. It's weird.

The mill owners sent them outside sometimes, when the machines broke down and work had to stop while the mechanics struggled to mend them. While the noisy machines were silenced, beneath the shroud of smoke, the cool, dank air came alive with gossip. Now and again she caught her name on people's lips. Everyone seemed to be talking about her, but no one would speak to her directly now that they knew her disgrace. She gazed at the girl she'd thought would always be her best friend, but the girl turned her back and went on gossiping to someone else. She'd never felt more alone than she did as she edged away from the chattering crowd. Behind the mill, beneath the rock face, a tangle of wild roses was blooming in a patch of smoky sunlight. The scent of the roses hung seductively in the heavy air. Now the morning waves of sickness had passed, she was hungry. Starving hungry. The plump, red rosehips looked ripe and tempting, good enough to eat.

Apart from the interesting stuff about the mill, it's been a stinky day, and by the end of it, I'm not feeling too good. It must be the lack of lunch – either that, or the packet of mints I found in the fluff at the bottom of my backpack. I've been sucking them all afternoon to try to block out the smell of the roses. Ma Harding's maths lesson didn't help take my mind off things, either. I'm feeling sick and wobbly. As I stuff things into my backpack, I pluck up courage and ask Alex to walk back home with me.

"I would if I could," he grins, as he hurries away clutching his kit bag, "but I've got a football match after school."

There's no point in asking Riya – she shot off the instant the bell went for the end of school. She and her little sister are probably back home already. There's not really anyone else to ask. Riya and I used to do everything together, so neither of us have, I mean *had*, much room for other friends. I could call Mum or Dad, of course, but then they'll rush up to school, all worried, and make a fuss, and that's the last thing I want.

I drag myself, and my backpack, to the girls' toilets. No one is around as I turn on a tap and splash water all over my face and the floor. My hair gets soaked in the process, and

I throw it back from my face and look in the mirror. Sad, hazel eyes in a very pale face framed by long, straggly blonde hair, stare unblinkingly back at me. The girl in the mirror looks vaguely familiar but, for a moment, I don't recognise her as me.

I'm not that surprised because right now, I don't feel much like me, either. I feel so alone. I close my eyes and open them. The girl in the mirror blinks back. Then I smile a watery smile at myself, rearrange my hair, and rub my cheeks with a paper towel until they turn pink. That's better. I'm me again. I'll be OK. It's not as if anything bad is going to happen on such a bright, sunny day, is it? There's no mountain to climb, it's downhill all the way back. Even so, I'll be very glad to get home to Mum. This smell is really getting to me now. I hoist my backpack over one shoulder and set off for the stepping stones.

She tried to swallow, but the dry, scratchy rosehips stuck in the back of her throat. The cough took hold of her again, rattling every bone in her fragile body. A long whistle blasted the still air, and the clanking machines started up again. She retched and gasped for breath as the mill workers poured back inside the mill. If she went back in there, she would suffocate. She had to get back to the cleaner air of the village, but she could hardly stand. How was she going to make it up the hill? If only she had a friend to help her up the stepping stones.

Down the stepping stones to home. Trudging slowly, step by step. The whole path stinks of roses. Putrid, mildewed roses. The smell's so bad it makes me want to throw up. I choke back the vomit, but I still can't work out where it's coming from. Where on earth are these roses? Half way down the hill, I dump my backpack on the ground and stop for a moment to look for them. It's cold all of a sudden and the air is still, not a breath of wind. All the birds have gone silent. Even the insects have stopped buzzing. There it is again. A low, moaning, gasping noise. The hairs on my forearms stand to attention and chills run up and down my spine. There's no one else around. It can't be me... can it?

The pain in her chest was crushing. She could hardly breathe. Step by agonising step, she placed her clogs in the worn-down hollows of the stepping stones and forced her shaking, aching body up them. Half-way up the hill, there was a thicket of roses. If only she could reach it, she'd rest awhile. There she would wait for someone to help her up the stepping stones.

My stomach's aching and I feel so cold and empty. If only Riya was with me. I hate not having a friend. All of a sudden my legs have gone all wobbly on me. I've got to rest here for a bit. Look! There are the roses! They're growing all around me. Funny I've never noticed them before. How could I ever have thought they were disgusting? They look gorgeous, and their scent is just heavenly. I stretch out my hand to cup a rose, but its perfect, waxy, pink petals crumble at my touch. The sickly sweet stench of decay wells up around me. I gasp, and my lungs fill with the fusty, musty dust.

My chest! It's being crushed!

Choking…

can't breathe…

Reach for inhaler. Why won't my arms move? Someone's holding them! Who on earth?

It's OK! I know her from somewhere! I'm remembering! She's hugging me…

calling my name …

telling me hers…

"*Rose!* Rose!"

I sensed it the instant she set foot upon the stepping stones. She smelled of roses. I knew that one day she would come and be my friend. Together, we can help each other up and down the stepping stones … and together, we can find more friends…

About the Author

Jane has been an archaeologist, a teacher and a library assistant, but is now a full-time children's writer with over 20 published books, plus poems in many children's anthologies.

Her picture books include *Gilbert the Great*, *Knight Time*, *Stuck in the Mud*, and her chapter books include *Dino Dog*, *No Nits*! and *Eye, Eye, Captain*! She also writes for the series **Dinosaur Cove**.

Jane lives near the White Cliffs of Dover, and enjoys visiting schools to share her love of writing. This is Jane's first collection of ghost stories, and she hopes they send shivers down your spine.

Other White Wolves Short Stories
From Different Fiction Genres...

DARK
EAGLE

AND OTHER HISTORICAL STORIES

Neil Tonge

A brother and sister suffer the harsh
conditions of the Victorian workhouse,
a boy is torn between loyalty to his
own clan and the occupying Romans,
two children are accidentally left
behind in occupied France...

Dark Eagle is a collection of short
stories from the historical genre.

ISBN: 978 0 7136 8904 4   £4.99

Other White Wolves Short Stories From Different Fiction Genres...

SPACE PIRATES

AND OTHER SCI-FI STORIES

Tony Bradman

Two children learn to survive in a lonely post-apocalyptic city, a boy attempts to outwit the most notorious pirate in the galaxy, a family try to make life work on a new planet after Earth is destroyed...

Space Pirates is a collection of short stories from the sci-fi genre.

ISBN: 978 0 7136 8905 1   £4.99

Titles available for Year 6